What's the Weather Like?

It's Cloudy

Celeste Bishop

illustrated by
Maria José Da Luz

PowerKiDS press.

New York

Published in 2017 by The Rosen Publishing Group, Inc.
29 East 21st Street, New York, NY 10010

First Edition

Managing Editor: Nathalie Beullens-Maoui
Editor: Sarah Machajewski
Book Design: Michael Flynn
Illustrator: Maria José Da Luz

Cataloging-in-Publication Data

Names: Bishop, Celeste.
Title: It's cloudy / Celeste Bishop.
Description: New York : Powerkids Press, 2016. | Series: What's the weather like? | Includes index.
Identifiers: ISBN 9781508152330 (pbk.) | ISBN 9781508152347 (library bound) | ISBN 9781499423020 (6 pack)
Subjects: LCSH: Clouds–Juvenile literature.
Classification: LCC QC921.35 B57 2016 | DDC 551.57'6–dc23

Manufactured in the United States of America

CPSIA Compliance Information: Batch #BS16PK: For Further Information contact Rosen Publishing, New York, New York at 1-800-237-9932

Contents

I can't see the sun today.

It's cloudy.

When it's cloudy, the sky is covered with clouds.

Some clouds are white and puffy.

I think they look like pillows!

Other clouds are dark and flat.

These clouds are a sign of rain.

The clouds are getting darker.
I think it's going to rain.

13

My mom says I can play outside until it rains.

I wear rain boots
just in case.

15

The clouds hide the sun.
I can't see my shadow!

The clouds are getting darker.
It starts to get windy, too.

It's time to go inside.

My mom says cloudy days
are perfect for reading.

It stays cloudy all day.

What will the weather
be like tomorrow?

23

Words to Know

pillows

rain

rain boots

Index